FRANKLIN STREET

Cabinetmaker

STREET

Printing Office and
Bookbindery

The Golden Ball
(Silversmith)

Raleigh Tavern

Pasteur & Galt
Apothecary Shop

Capitol

GLOUCESTER STREET

King's Arms Barber Shop
(Wigmaker)

James Anderson
Blacksmith Shop

Ayscough House
(Gunsmith)

STREET

BOTETOURT STREET

WALLER STREET

YORK STREET

D Is for Drums

A Colonial Williamsburg ABC

Kay Chorao

Harry N. Abrams, Inc., Publishers
in association with The Colonial Williamsburg Foundation

is for Apothecary shop
and Aprons.

is for Blacksmith, Broom,
Beds, and Baskets.

is for Capitol, Cooper, Cradle, Cat, Clocked stockings, Churn, and Chairs.

is for Dolls, Drums, and Dresses.

is for Embroidery, Eggs,
Ewe, and Engraving.

is for Fireplace, Floorcloth,
Frock coat, and Fan.

is for Gunsmith, Goose,
Goat, and Gate.

is for Hoops, Hospital,
Harness, and Horses.

is for Icehouse, Ivy, Ink balls,
and Inkstand.

is for Justice, Jugglers,
and Jack-in-the-box.

is for Kitchen, Kittens,
Kettle, and Kerchief.

is for Lion, Loom,
Lambs, and Lanterns.

is for Magazine, Musician,
Marbles, and Maze.

is for Nest, Necessary,
and Necklaces.

dovecote

smokehouse

dairy

kitchen and well

chicken coop

stable

is for Outbuildings.

is for **Palace**, **Plates**, and **Parish**.

is for Queen, Quoits, Quills, and Quilt.

is for Rake, Rooster, Racing,
and Riding chair.

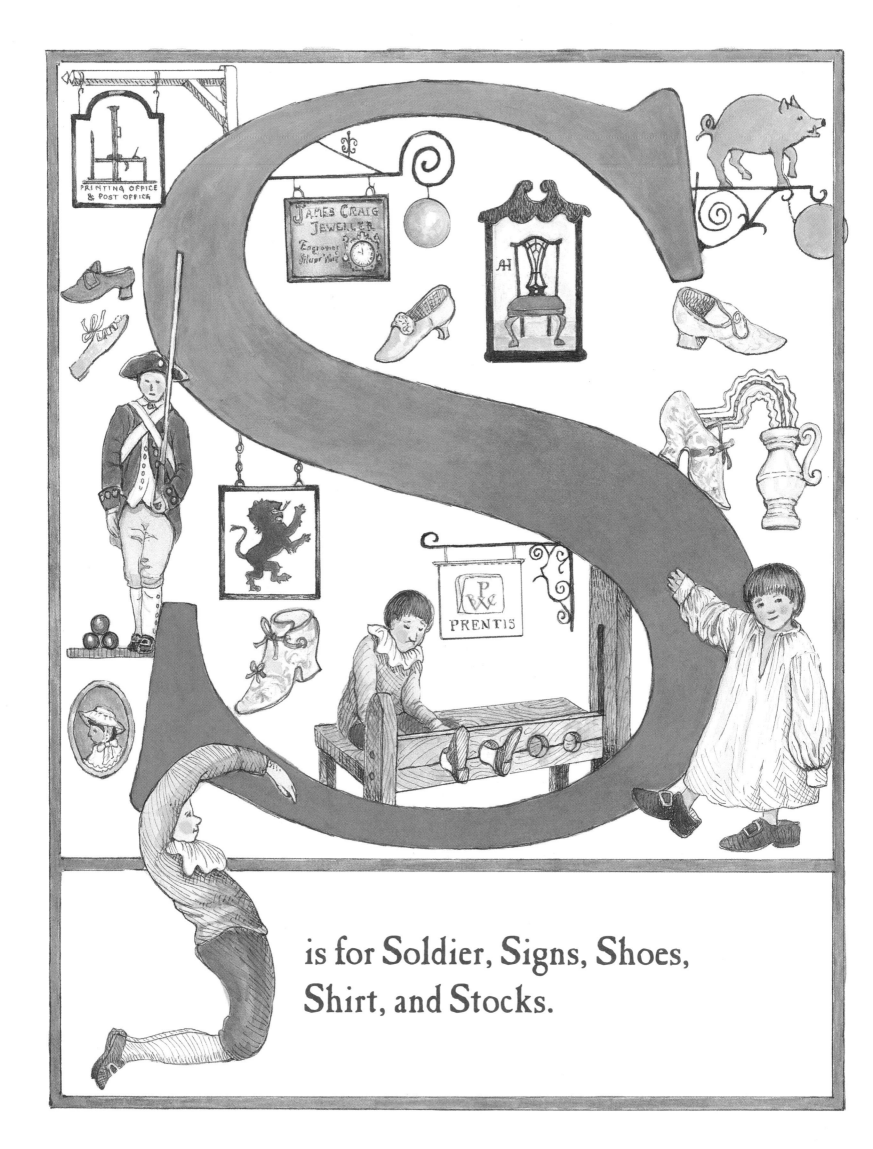

is for Soldier, Signs, Shoes,
Shirt, and Stocks.

is for Toys, Tavern, and Tailor.

is for Undergarments
and Unicorns.

is for **Vegetable garden,**
Vines, and **Virginia.**

is for Windmill, Wigs,
Wigmaker, and Wagon.

is for signed with an **X**.
Can you find the other Xs?

is for Yoke, Yarn, Yarrow, and Yawn.

is for Zeke and Zack the oxen.

Glossary

A

Apothecary shop: An apothecary shop in colonial times was a pharmacy or drugstore where you could buy drugs and herbal remedies. You could also visit the doctor there. The Pasteur & Galt Apothecary Shop in Virginia's colonial capital, Williamsburg, was run by two doctor-apothecaries who could perform surgery and even deliver babies!

Aprons: There were a great variety of aprons in colonial times, and they were worn by children, ladies, servants, and even gentlemen when they had their wigs powdered.

B

Baskets: In colonial times, baskets were everywhere. People used them as shopping bags, tote bags, and purses. They were perfect for carrying bread, vegetables, and other foods to and from market, and for transporting live poultry, gathering eggs, and carrying needlework and books.

Beds: Colonial beds could look grand, with tall, fabric-covered high posts, or plain, with just wooden posts. The mattresses often rested on frames crisscrossed with ropes. Many people had no bedstead at all.

Blacksmith: A colonial blacksmith made tools, rims for wheels, nails, fireplace pokers, tongs, andirons (metal racks that hold logs in a fireplace), and other useful household items. At the James Anderson Blacksmith Shop in Colonial Williamsburg's Historic Area, you can see smiths working in the traditional way.

C

Capitol: This Williamsburg building was the seat of government for the colony of Virginia where men elected by free, white property owners or chosen by the King of England made laws to regulate life in Virginia. The Capitol also held a courtroom where those laws could be enforced.

Chairs: Some of the finest furniture in the thirteen colonies was made in Williamsburg, in Hay's Cabinetmaking Shop. Cabinetmakers built not only chairs, tables, and bookcases, but also fancy garden fences, harpsichords, and coffins!

Clocked stockings: These stockings, worn by gentlemen, were named for the design running up the legs. "Clocked" meant flowered or inverted work about the ankle.

Cooper: Coopers built casks, including barrels and churns for making butter, buckets, and other wooden household containers. They traveled from place to place, wherever their work was needed. Large plantations often trained slaves to produce the casks needed to store tobacco.

Cradle: Colonial babies slept in cradles, not cribs. A busy mother could use her foot to rock her baby to sleep.

D

Dolls: Most colonial dolls were carved of wood and painted. Some had jointed arms and legs made of wood. Most had wooden bodies. Fancier versions were owned by wealthy girls whose families had the dolls imported from England. But plain or fancy, the dolls were probably loved equally well.

Dresses: Dresses were called gowns in the eighteenth century. The gowns colonial women wore said something about who they were. Wealthy women might wear gowns made of fine English silk, while poorer women wore gowns of inexpensive cloth.

Drums: Drums were signal instruments for the infantry, relaying orders to soldiers in camp and in battle. They also supplied rhythm for marching. The music was a way of telling soldiers the duties of the day, how fast to march, and in which direction to move while in combat.

E

Embroidery: Embroidery is the process of stitching decorative patterns, alphabets, and sometimes numbers onto a fabric using a needle and thread. The art of embroidery reached great heights in the eighteenth century. The exquisite hand stitching transformed ladies' gowns and men's coats and waistcoats into works of art. You can see some examples in the Museums of Colonial Williamsburg.

Engraving: Engraving was the work of silversmiths who decorated trays and teapots and a wide variety of household pieces by cutting patterns or words into metal.

Ewe: A ewe is a female sheep. Sheep supplied meat and wool to colonial families. Wool could be spun into yarn and thread for clothes and blankets. Sheep still live in Colonial Williamsburg's Historic Area where rare breeds such as Leicester Longwools are raised.

F

Fan: Carried by ladies, fans weren't just for keeping cool. They were an accessory, like jewelry, and useful for emphasizing a gesture or hiding behind when feeling shy or coy.

Fireplace: Found in every colonial home from humble to noble, fireplaces provided warmth for comfort and cooking.

Floorcloth: A floorcloth was a covering that might be painted to resemble something finer, such as marble.

Frock coat: Colonial men wore these garments for work and informal activities.

G

Gunsmith: A gunsmith turned iron, steel, brass, and wood into rifles and other firearms, which could be used for hunting or in battle. Today, smiths at the Ayscough House in Colonial Williamsburg's Historic Area fashion firearms in the colonial manner.

H

Hoops: Rolling a hoop with a stick was a favorite playtime activity of colonial children.

Hospital: The Public Hospital in Williamsburg was built for the care of the mentally ill only, and was the first of its kind in America.

Hotch Potch: Hotch Potch is an eighteenth-century children's character who was also called "Posture Master" because he could twist and turn his body into any letter of the alphabet. He appeared on prints and handkerchiefs of the time and became popular in England and colonial America, and was most likely used by children to learn the alphabet.

I

Icehouse: A place for storing ice, an icehouse could be either a pit or a structure built into a hillside or covered by a mound. Ice was cut from ponds during the winter and used to keep food cool in a time when there were no refrigerators.

Ink balls: Ink balls were used by the printer to apply ink to trays of metal type. The printer then put the trays into a printing press, which literally "pressed" paper to the ink-stained type. You can see printers at work at the Printing Office in Colonial Williamsburg's Historic Area.

Inkstand: An inkstand was a metal or wooden tray or box with compartments for ink, quills, blotting sand, and sealing wax.

J

Jack-in-the-box: This toy was made as early as the sixteenth century to entertain children. A puppetlike character popped up from a decorated box to squeals of delighted surprise.

Jugglers: In colonial times, traveling theater troupes that included jugglers would move from town to town, providing entertainment for the public.

Justice: A justice was a judge. He presided over trials of those who were accused of wrongdoing.

K

Kerchief: A kerchief was a triangular or folded square piece of cloth worn over a woman's shoulders.

Kitchen: In the colonial capital, kitchens were usually set apart from main houses to keep heat, cooking smells, and threat of fire at a distance. The outbuilding also separated slaves and servants from the gentry they served.

L

Lanterns: With no streetlights, colonists needed lanterns to see their way at night.

Lion: The lion that decorates the front of the Governor's Palace in Colonial Williamsburg's Historic Area is a symbol of the British crown. Virginia was once a colony of Great Britain, which is why its early history is called "colonial."

Loom: A loom was a large wooden structure on which men and women wove wool, linen, and cotton into cloth that would then be made into clothes or textiles to furnish their homes.

M

Magazine: A magazine was a building where an army or militia stored its gunpowder, firearms, and other equipment.

Maze: Made of carefully clipped shrubs, mazes were grown for the amusement of ladies and gentlemen in England. The maze at the Governor's Palace in Colonial Williamsburg's Historic Area is based on English examples.

N

Necessary: This was a well-named building, which we would call an outhouse. It was truly necessary in a time before toilets and plumbing.

O

Outbuildings: Outbuildings were not connected to the main house. Outbuildings could include stables, kitchens, smokehouses (where meat or fish were cured), and, of course, necessaries.

P

Palace: The Governor's Palace was the most elegant residence in Williamsburg where the governor of the Virginia colony lived.

Parish: Bruton Parish Church in Williamsburg is one of the oldest churches in continuous use since colonial times. Thomas Jefferson, Patrick Henry, and George Washington worshipped there.

Plates: Plates could be made of porcelain, earthenware, pewter, or wood. The finest porcelain ones came from as far away as China and were called "China ware."

Q

Queen: A portrait of Queen Charlotte, wife of King George III of Britain, hangs in the Governor's Palace ballroom in Colonial Williamsburg's Historic Area.

Quills: These were pens made of cleaned bird feathers cut in the shape of a nib that could be dipped in an inkwell and used to write words on paper.

Quoits: Quoits was a colonial game of ringtoss.

R

Racing: Horse racing was a popular colonial sport. The jockeys were usually young black men or boys.

Riding chair: Smaller than a carriage, a riding chair is a two-wheeled, single horse-drawn vehicle for one or two people. Most colonists traveled by foot or horseback. Only the wealthy could afford carriages or riding chairs.

Rooster: Colonists kept hens and roosters for meat, eggs, and sport. You can still find roosters such as the Silver-Spangled Hamburg in Colonial Williamsburg's Historic Area where they are raised as part of the rare breeds program.

S

Signs: In colonial times, shops had signs with pictures as well as words so the many colonists who could not read would still know which shop sold what.

Stocks: Stocks rhymes with socks, and both are for your feet. Being sent to the stocks was like being sent to your room, but worse because everyone in town could watch you sitting, legs trapped, through the duration of your punishment. You might be sent to the stocks for being rude to the justice. Today, you can try out the stocks outside the Courthouse in Colonial Williamsburg's Historic Area.

T

Tailor: Just as today, a tailor measured customers and made clothes to fit them. He repaired clothes, too.

Tavern: A tavern was a social gathering place for locals and a sort of rest stop for travelers. The Raleigh Tavern still stands on Duke of Gloucester Street in Colonial Williamsburg's Historic Area.

Toys: Colonial children had few toys, but some they might have had include dolls and wooden pull-toys.

U

Undergarments: Men's shirts were cut long enough to serve as underwear, but women had many undergarments. Stays were laced and stiffened garments worn under the bodice of a gown. They were believed to give good posture. Pockets were sewn to a tape and tied under the skirt (they could be reached through slits in the skirt). Petticoats were full underskirts, sometimes worn two at a time. Shifts were knee-length white linen or cotton garments with three-quarter-length sleeves. They were worn beneath all the other layers.

Unicorns

Unicorns: Next to the lion on the front of the Governor's Palace in Colonial Williamsburg's Historic Area is a unicorn, symbol of Great Britain, the former ruler of Virginia and all thirteen American colonies.

V

Vegetable garden: Many colonists grew their own vegetables in small gardens near their kitchens.

Virginia: Williamsburg was once the capital of Virginia when it was still a colony of Great Britain.

W

Wigs: Colonial men of social standing wore wigs in polite society. Wigs were made of human hair or other materials, such as goat or horse hair. They were made in a variety of colors and often powdered to enhance their color and add a nice scent.

Windmill: A windmill ground grains of various kinds when its four giant blades with canvas "sails" caught the wind and turned the grinding mechanism. Today, you can see the reconstructed Robertson's Windmill in Colonial Williamsburg's Historic Area.

X

Signed with an X: Many colonists did not know how to write their own names. They would sign documents with an X.

Y

Yarn: In colonial times, yarn was made on a spinning wheel, which twisted sheep's wool, linen, or cotton into thin threads.

Yarrow: This flower was grown in colonial gardens and used as a medicinal herb. People applied it to wounds and used it to break fevers.

Yoke: A yoke is a frame fitted to a person's shoulders to carry a load in two equal portions.

Z

Zeke and Zack: These are the names of a fine pair of Devon oxen, part of the rare breeds program in Colonial Williamsburg's Historic Area.

Author's Note

My first vague notions of creating *D Is for Drums: A Colonial Williamsburg ABC* were fanciful visions of animals in eighteenth-century garb: perhaps a gentleman cow in waistcoat writing with a quill or a mouse in buckle shoes rolling a hoop or a dog in flowing gown spinning yarn.

Then I visited Colonial Williamsburg's Historic Area.

I walked about. The animals I found included gleaming horses pulling carriages, a pair of yoked oxen, rare sheep and chickens of eighteenth-century lineage, and an ordinary barn cat, calmly observing coopers. All these animals blended into the colonial setting with quiet dignity and purpose. The buildings, fences, fields, and gardens that surrounded them were simple and elegant.

My first whimsical visions melted away. I met with staff members of The Colonial Williamsburg Foundation. They were caring and protective of this special place, and all the elements that compose the whole. The book concept was up to me, but they preferred as many images as possible for each letter. We all wanted this book to reflect the unique details that form this window into the past.

At home I pondered. One of my favorite discoveries in Williamsburg was the Hotch Potch figure. In The DeWitt Wallace Decorative Arts Museum I had tracked down his earliest representation on an eighteenth-century handkerchief. I had purchased a set of Posture Master Alphabet cards from the gift shop; I spread them out on a table. Each card was a Hotch Potch figure bent to represent a letter of the alphabet (except J and U, which only came into general use in the nineteenth century). Hotch Potch was educational and even whimsical in his own eighteenth-century way. He became the starting point for my book. He would appear on every page, both as himself and again in the large panel, like an actor floating among stage props.

The large capital letters on each page are of eighteenth-century design, as are the simple borders, borrowed from the Posture Master Alphabet cards, which were adapted from the print published in 1782 by Carington Bowles.

My hope is that children will view this book as a treasure hunt and an introduction to eighteenth-century words and images. All the objects, buildings, and details are as faithful to Colonial Williamsburg's Historic Area as possible, with just a few flights of fancy.

—Kay Chorao

To all the Colonial Williamsburg scholars who work with such dedication to uncover and preserve an authentic view of our American past, and with special appreciation to Erin Michaela Bendiner. —K.C.

Designer: Edward Miller

Library of Congress Cataloging-in-Publication Data:

Chorao, Kay.
  D Is for Drums : A Colonial Williamsburg A.B.C. / Kay Chorao.
    p. cm.
  ISBN 0-8109-4927-X (Abrams) — ISBN 0-87935-197-7 (The Colonial Williamsburg Foundation)
1. Colonial Williamsburg (Williamsburg, Va.)—Juvenile literature. 2. Williamsburg (Va.)—History—Juvenile literature. 3. English language—Alphabet—Juvenile literature. [1. Colonial Williamsburg (Williamsburg, Va.) 2. Williamsburg (Va.)—History. 3. Alphabet.]
I. Title.

  F234.W7C52 2004
  975.5'425202—dc22

 2003025793

Published in 2004 by Harry N. Abrams, Incorporated, New York

Printed and bound in China

10 9 8 7 6 5 4 3 2 1

ABRAMS Harry N. Abrams, Inc.
        100 Fifth Avenue
        New York, NY 10011
        www.abramsbooks.com

Abrams is a subsidiary of

LA MARTINIÈRE
        GROUPE

Colonial Williamsburg
The Colonial Williamsburg Foundation
Williamsburg, Virginia
www.colonialwilliamsburg.org

From 1699 to 1780, Williamsburg was the capital of England's oldest, largest, richest, and most populous colony. Today, the restored Historic Area is owned and operated by The Colonial Williamsburg Foundation, a private, not-for-profit educational institution whose goal is to engage and inspire people to learn about this important chapter in American history.

Your purchase of this book helps support the Foundation's ongoing mission to preserve and restore eighteenth-century Williamsburg . . . that the future may learn from the past.

To learn more about visiting Colonial Williamsburg call 1-800-HISTORY (447-8679) or visit our Web site at www.colonialwilliamsburg.com, or shop with us at www.williamsburgmarketplace.com.

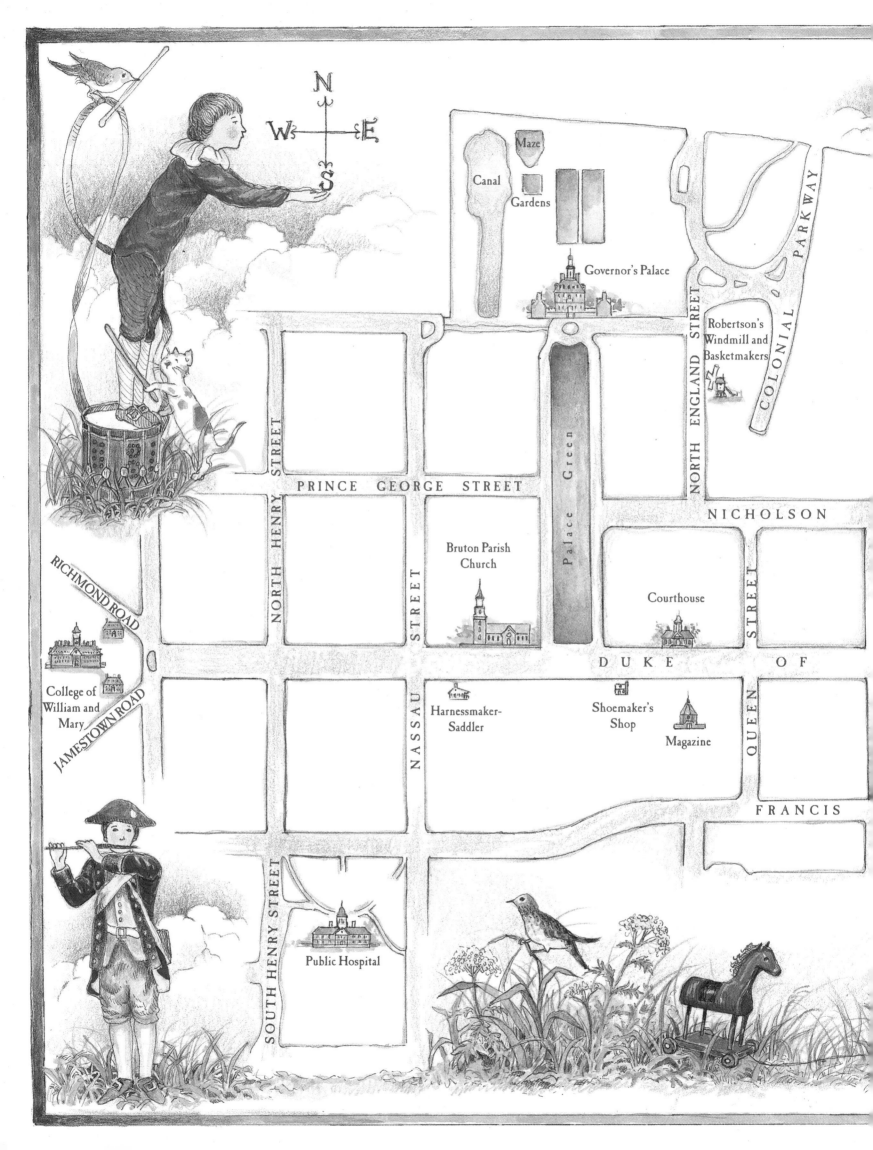